THE UNICORN MIX-UP

More **ROYALLY EXCITING ADVENTURES** to look out for:

THE ENCHANTED FOREST

THE BIG BAD SNOWY DAY

THE BEST PRINCESS

written by
KiRSTY APPLEBAUM

illustrated by
SAHAR HAGHGOO

PRiNCESS MiNNA

THE UNICORN MIX-UP

nosy crow

First published in the UK in 2022 by Nosy Crow Ltd
The Crow's Nest, 14 Baden Place,
Crosby Row, London, SE1 1YW, UK

Nosy Crow Eireann Ltd
44 Orchard Grove, Kenmare,
Co Kerry, V93 FY22, Ireland

Nosy Crow and associated logos are trademarks and/or registered
trademarks of Nosy Crow Ltd.

ISBN: 978 1 78800 975 1

A CIP catalogue record for this book will be available from the British Library.

Printed and bound in China.

Papers used by Nosy Crow are made from wood grown in sustainable forests.

1 3 5 7 9 10 8 6 4 2

www.nosycrow.com

FOR DENNIS
K. A.

Chapter One

This is Minna. She is a **princess**.
Princess Minna is very good at
lots of things.

She is good at taming unicorns,
kissing frogs and fighting dragons.

Sometimes, she can tell if there is a pea under a mattress just by lying on it. One tiny pea can make a princess toss and turn all night. But you don't get many peas under mattresses these days.

Princess Minna lives in

Castle Tall-Towers

with the King, the Queen and a wizard called Raymond.

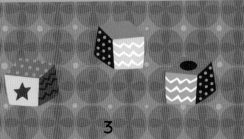

When all is well in the kingdom, lots of grey doves **sweep** and **swoop** around the towers making soft cooing noises. They make the whole castle smell like tutti-frutti ice cream.

When all is **not** well in the kingdom, big seagulls fly up from the coast and scare the doves away.

Then they **flip** and **flap** around the towers, making **screechy squawking** noises.

They make the whole castle smell like old seaweed.

There are also blackbirds at Castle Tall-Towers. They don't make the castle smell of anything. No one takes much notice of them.

One morning, Princess Minna woke up feeling **very** tired.

She had not slept well **at all**.

Perhaps there was a pea under her mattress.

But, no, she thought. It couldn't be that. You **never** find peas under mattresses anymore.

Flip! Flap! Flap! Flip!

Princess Minna looked out of the window.

Screech! Squawk!

Squawk! Screech!

Oh dear. The seagulls were back and the doves were nowhere to be seen.

All is **not** well in the kingdom, thought Princess Minna. I'd better go and tell the others.

Princess Minna's bedroom is right at the top of this tower here. It takes her a **very long time** to get downstairs.

She ran **down**
and **down**
and **down**

and **down**
and **down**
and **down**
and **down**
and **down**
and **down**

until she reached the dining room,
where everyone else was having
breakfast.

Princess Minna was **even** more tired now, and **very** out of breath. "All is **not** well," she huffed and puffed. "The doves have gone and the seagulls are back!"

"**Oh dear**," said the Queen. "That explains why my tea has feathers in it."

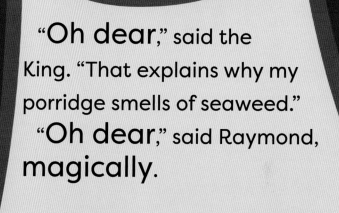

"Oh dear," said the King. "That explains why my porridge smells of seaweed."

"Oh dear," said Raymond, magically.

"Never mind," said the King. "I'm sure Minna can sort it out."

Hurrah! thought Princess Minna. She loved sorting out the kingdom. What would it be this time?

A unicorn in need of taming?

A **frog** waiting to be kissed?

A **dragon** looking for a fight?

"Please be quick, Minna," said the Queen. "The King and I have invited Lord and Lady Welling-Tunboot round to play **musical statues** this afternoon."

"It's been planned for weeks," said the King. "But we won't be able to do it if the castle is full of seagulls..."

"...and then where will we be?" said the Queen.

Princess Minna was already on her way. She **ran** out of

Castle Tall-Towers

towards the town, shooing a few blackbirds away as she went.

Chapter Two

The townspeople **loved** Princess Minna. They were very pleased to see her.

They brought out their **babies** to be kissed, because princesses **always** like kissing babies.

They quickly baked some **sponge cakes** with cream in the middle, because princesses **always** enjoy a nice piece of sponge cake with cream in the middle.

They climbed wobbly ladders to pin up **bunting**, because princesses **always** feel happy when there's bunting out.

23

Princess Minna was really **very** tired now, but she still managed to **kiss** a few babies, eat some cake and admire the bunting.

Afterwards, she pointed towards the castle. "Look," she said. "All is **not** well in the kingdom. There are seagulls flying around the towers and the doves are nowhere to be seen."

The townspeople looked. They saw the seagulls. They scratched their heads and wondered what could be wrong. Everything seemed perfectly fine.

Suddenly there was a **crash!**
"Help! Help!
We have a

unicorn
emergency!"

Everyone turned round.
It was Little Tommy
Turret from Turret's
T shop.

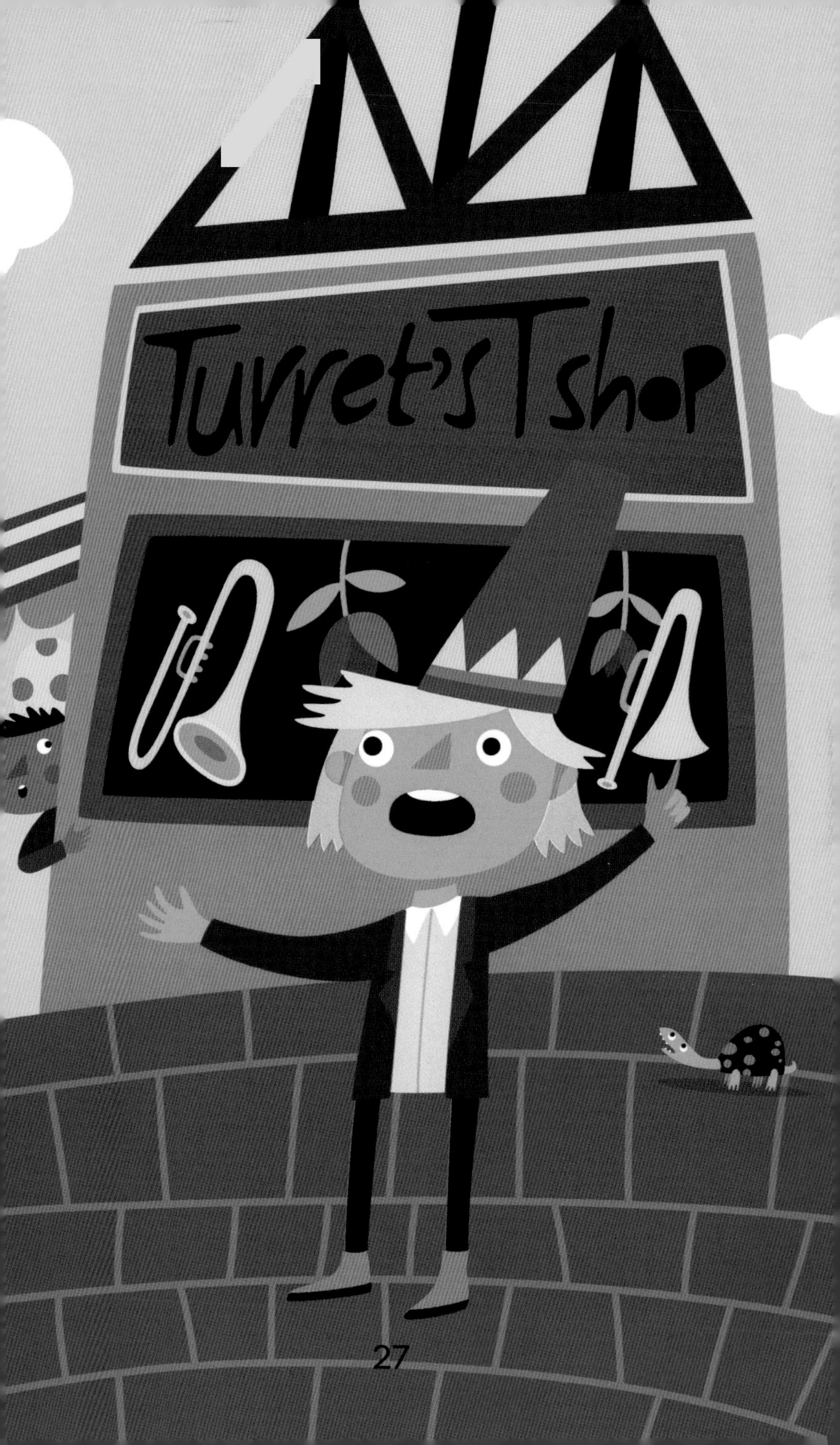
Turret's T shop

You can buy tea in Turret's T
shop. You can also buy towels
and trombones and trousers and
tulips and everything else you can
possibly think of that begins with T.
But you can't buy pterodactyls

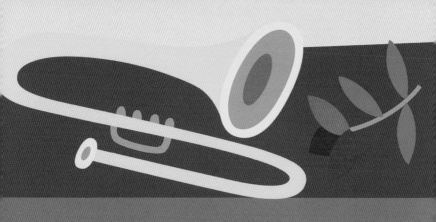

there even though it sounds like
you should be able to.
   But back to the

unicorn
emergency.

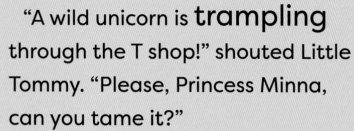

"A wild unicorn is **trampling** through the T shop!" shouted Little Tommy. "Please, Princess Minna, can you tame it?"

Princess Minna smiled. This must be the reason for the seagulls.

She just needed to tame the unicorn and **all** would be well in the kingdom once more. Taming unicorns was one of her **special skills.**

Surely she wasn't **too** tired for that!

Princess Minna strode over to
Turret's T shop.

"Throw me my **trusty sword**,"
she called.

The townspeople were confused.
Princess Minna only ever called for

her **trusty sword** when she was
going to fight a dragon, not when
she was going to tame a unicorn.

But someone threw her a **trusty
sword** anyway. Princess Minna
caught it with one hand.

There was a **clang** as the sword **banged** against the unicorn's horn.

There was an

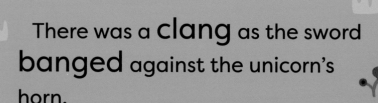

as the unicorn swished its tail into Princess Minna's eyes.

There was an

as the unicorn stood on Princess Minna's toes.

Princess Minna was **fighting** the unicorn instead of **taming** it! It turned out that Princess Minna was not very good at fighting unicorns. But it didn't matter because unicorns are not all that interested in fighting. After a while they just get bored and run off.

"Oh dear," said Princess Minna,
rubbing her toes. "I don't know
what came over me."
She yawned

a very big yawn.

Chapter
Three

Suddenly there was a **ribbet!**
"Help! Help!

We have a

frog emergency!"

It was Little Pippi Piper from Piper's P shop. You can buy peas in Piper's P shop. You can even buy pterodactyls there, as it happens.

But back to the

frog emergency.

40

"Princess Minna," said Little Pippi, "we have a frog that needs kissing. Can you help?"

She held out the frog to Princess Minna.

Princess Minna smiled. This must be the reason for the seagulls. She just needed to kiss the frog and all would be well in the kingdom once more. Kissing frogs was one of her

special skills.

Surely she wasn't too tired for that!

But instead of **kissing** the frog,
Princess Minna started to **stroke**
it and **whisper** in
its ear.

The townspeople were confused again. Princess Minna only ever **stroked and whispered** when she was taming unicorns, not when she was kissing frogs.

Princess Minna was **taming** the frog instead of **kissing** it!

The frog started to get annoyed. It wanted to turn back into a handsome prince. Eventually it **hopped** away.

"Oh dear," said Princess Minna, shaking her head. "I'm **incredibly** tired. It's making me get everything

terribly mixed up."

45

Suddenly there was a **roar!**
"Help! Help!
We have a **dragon**
emergency!"

It was Little Betty Button from
Button's B shop. You can buy
books and bananas and bicycles in
Button's B shop.

"Look!" said Little Betty.

Button's B
Shop

The townspeople turned round to see **a terrifying dragon** breathing fire over the rooftops. Some people screamed. Some people fainted. But Princess Minna smiled. This must be the **real** reason for the seagulls! She just needed to fight the dragon and all would be well in the kingdom once more.

Fighting dragons was one of her

special skills.

Surely she wasn't **too** tired for that!

She pursed her lips and started running towards the **fiery beast**.

"Hold on," said Little Betty (who was quite clever).

"If Princess Minna has been trying to **fight the unicorn** and **tame the frog,** that means she's going to ... **kiss the dragon!**"

"We have to stop her!"
cried the townspeople.
But it was **too** late.

Princess Minna had already clambered on to the dragon's back. Now she was planting a big, smickery-smackery kiss on his scaly, blue cheek.

The townspeople held their breath.

They waited for the dragon to toss Princess Minna into the air, catch her in his scissory teeth and swallow her whole.

"What will we tell the Queen?" they whispered.

"What will we tell the King?"

"What will we tell Raymond?"

They covered their faces. They couldn't bear to watch.

Chapter
Four

The townspeople peeped through their fingers.

There was Princess Minna, still clinging to the dragon's neck.

The dragon smiled **a big, dragony smile.**

Then he gave a big, dragony

roar.

This time, though, it was a happy

roar.

57

"Oh, Princess Minna!" said the dragon. "You are the first person ever to kiss me apart from my mum. From now on I will be your **best friend in the whole world** and I promise to stay by your side **for ever and ever** and even a bit longer if I possibly can.

And just so you know, my name is **Lorenzo,** which is actually a very popular name for dragons at the moment. I have two cousins in neighbouring kingdoms who are also called Lorenzo."

Lorenzo crouched down so that
Princess Minna could climb off.
The townspeople stopped
holding their breath. They were

amazed.

They didn't even know dragons
could speak. They started to
celebrate.

There is nothing townspeople like
better than a good celebration.

But Princess Minna didn't feel like celebrating. She sat on the ground and put her head in her hands. Her **heavy, sleepy eyelids** began to close.

The townspeople offered Princess Minna more cake but she said she wasn't hungry.

They brought their babies over for her to kiss but she shook her head. They pointed up at the bunting but it didn't make her feel happy. Princess Minna was **very sad.**

Maybe she would **never** sleep well again.

Maybe she would **always** be this tired now and her **special skills** would **always** be mixed up.

Maybe she had

tamed her last unicorn,

kissed her last frog and

fought her last dragon.

Maybe from now on she would have to do **boring** stuff in the castle like

polishing the crowns

and **dusting the thrones.**

Princess Minna gave a **big**, loud, tired **sigh**.

Princess Minna gave a **big**, loud, tired **sniff**.

She could hardly keep her eyes open.

"Lorenzo," she said. "I need to go to sleep. Could you take me back home?"

Lorenzo scooped Princess Minna carefully on to his back. She held on tight. He smelled of dragony things like **fire** and **smoke** and **fresh speckledy eggs**.

At least I've got a new friend, she thought.

Lorenzo unfolded his wings. He swung them up and swished them down.

Wallooop!

They flew high, high up into the sky.

Chapter
Five

The wind **whooshed** past
Princess Minna as they glided
towards **Castle Tall-Towers.**
It made her feel a bit more
awake.

Every so often, Lorenzo swung
and swished his wings again.

Wallooop

wallooop

wallooop!

Soon,

Castle
Tall-Towers

came into sight.

"What are those things
on my window ledge?" said
Princess Minna. She pointed to her
tower-top window.

Lorenzo flew closer.

"**Blackbirds!**" cried Princess
Minna. "But what have they got in
their beaks?"

Lorenzo flew up to the window, then twirled the ends of his wings around so that he hovered in one spot. Now Princess Minna could see the blackbirds more easily.

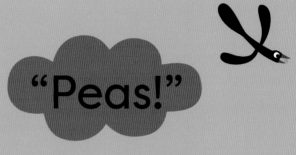

"Peas!"

she said. "They've got **peas** in their beaks!"

And you'll never guess what the blackbirds did next.

They flew into Princess Minna's room, poked the peas **under her mattress** and flew back out again.

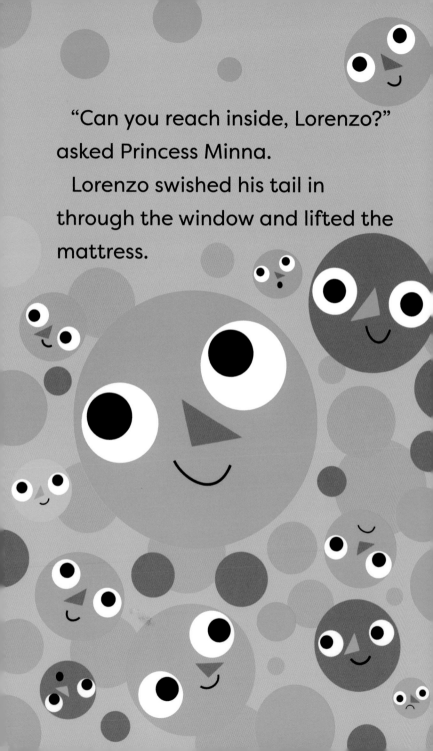

"Can you reach inside, Lorenzo?"
asked Princess Minna.

Lorenzo swished his tail in
through the window and lifted the
mattress.

There, underneath, were
hundreds of peas.
Maybe even

thousands.

Princess Minna's mouth dropped open **very wide indeed.**

The blackbirds must have been doing this for **days.**

One **tiny** pea under Princess Minna's mattress might make her toss and turn all night. But **this many** peas would mean she'd barely sleep **at all.**

No wonder she'd woken up tired. **No wonder** her

special skills

were all mixed up.

Lorenzo flew down and landed in front of **Castle Tall-Towers.**

Princess Minna
ran inside.
"Hello, Minna," said the
Queen, picking feathers
off the

royal sofa.

"Will the kingdom be sorted soon? The seagulls quite ruined my elevenses."

"Lord and Lady Welling-Tunboot will be here before we know it," said the King, cleaning seagull poo off the royal TV.

"Why is there a dragon on the lawn?" said Raymond, looking out of the royal window.

Princess Minna explained about the **blackbirds** and the **peas** and the **terrible mix-up**. Then she led everyone outside to meet Lorenzo.

"Very pleased to meet you," said the King.

"Very pleased to meet you too, Your Majesty," said Lorenzo.

"My mum sent me out into the world to make my fortune and she is **not** going to believe that I've met a **real princess** and a **real king** and a **real queen** and a **real wizard**.

Roar!"

Afterwards, Princess Minna gathered up all the peas from under her mattress. She put them into an **enormous** bin bag and took them to Piper's P shop. It seemed the best place for them.

The King gave the blackbirds a good telling-off. "Next time you're naughty you might get **baked in a pie**," he said.

"And then where will you be?" said the Queen.

The seagulls flew back to the coast and the doves returned to **Castle Tall-Towers**.

The King and Queen cleaned up the seagull feathers. Then they played musical statues with Lord and Lady Welling-Tunboot all afternoon.

89

Princess Minna snuggled up next to her new friend, Lorenzo. She fell into a **very good, very long** sleep with **no peas at all.**

The doves made soft cooing noises.

The castle smelled of tutti-frutti ice cream.

And **all** was well in the kingdom once more.